Two Princess and Other Santal Folk Tales

Two Princess and Other Santal Folk Tales

A. Campbell

HERITAGE

HERITAGE PUBLISHERS
New Delhi

First Published in 2026
by HERITAGE PUBLISHERS
19-A, Ansari Road, Daryaganj,
New Delhi -110 002
INDIA

Typeset in Times New Roman.

ISBN : 9788170265030

Printed and bound in India

Contents

Preface *vii*
The Story of Lelha 1
The Story of Sindura Gand Garur 35
The Tiger and Ulta's Mother 41
The Greatest Cheat of Seven 49
The Story of Two Princesses 55
Seven Brothers and their Sister 61
The Story of Jhore 68
The Girl who always found helpers 80
A Simple Thief 89

Preface

Of late years the Folk tales of India have been the subject of much study and research, and several interesting collections of them have been published. But I am not aware that as yet the folk lore of the Santals, has not received the attention which it deserved. The Santals as a people, have, to a remarkable degree, outside influences to which they have long been exposed, and to which such a large number of aboriginal tribes have succumbed. They have retained their language, institutions, tribal organization, and religion almost intact. Their traditions show the jealousy with which these have been guarded and the suspicion and distrust with which contact with their Aryan neighbours was regarded. The point at which they have been most accessible to outward influence and example, is in their relations with the aboriginal tribes, who in a more or less degree have merged themselves in Hinduism. Hindu ideas, customs and beliefs, filtering through these tribes, became considerably modified before they reached the Santals, and were therefore less potent in their effects than if they had been drawn from the fountain head of Hinduism itself. Still, in respect to their aboriginal neighbours they are always on their guard, ready to repel any innovation on their customs or religion with which they may be threatened. In the folk tales of such a people we may well expect to find something, if not altogether new, still interesting and instructive from an ethnological point of view, and this expectation, I believe, would be abundantly gratified if they were only made accessible to those who, by training and study, are competent to deal with them.

Santal folk-tales may be divided into two classes—those apparently purely Santal in their origin, and those obtained from other sources. Those of the first class are by far the more numerous, and besides showing the superstitious awe with which the Santals regard the creations of their own fancy, they throw a flood of light upon the social customs and usages of this most interesting people. The second class embraces a large number of the more popular tales current among the Hindus and semi-Hinduised aborigines. These, although adapted and modified by the Santals to suit their language, modes of thought, and social usages, may generally be detected by the presence of proper names, or untranslatable phrases which unmistakably indicate the source from which they have been derived.

These tales were taken down in Santali at first hand, and are therefore genuine and redolent of the soil. In translating them I have allowed myself considerable latitude without in any way diverging so far from the original as to in any degree impair their value to the student of Indian Folk-lore.

It was to be expected that in the popular tales of a simple, unpolished people like the Santals, expressions and allusions unfitted for ears polite would be found. In all such cases the changes which have been made are in accord with Santal thought and usage, so that the tales are, notwithstanding these alterations, thoroughly Santali.

I have aimed at making these Santal Folk-tales, in their English dress, true to the forests and hills of their nativity. I am not without hope, that in this I have succeeded in some small degree.

A number of the tales included in this volume have already appeared in the Indian Evangelical Review, but in this collected form they are more likely to prove of service to those who take an interest in the subject.

This volume of Santal Folk-Tales is offered as a humble contribution to the Folk-lore of India.

The Story of Lelha

I

There once lived a certain raja, who had three wives. The two elder had two sons each, and the younger only one, whose name was Lelha.[1] The four sons of the first two wives were very friendly with each other, being seldom separate, but they despised Lelha, and never permitted him to join them in any of their pastimes or sports.

The raja had a plot of ground set apart for a flower garden, but there was nothing in it. One day a certain Jugi came to him, and said, "Oh! raja, if you fill your

---

[1] Lelha in Santali means foolish.

garden with all kinds of flowering plants, your whole city will appear enchanting." Having said this, the Jugi went to his home. The raja was greatly affected by what the Jugi had said, and was immediately seized with a fit of the sulks. There was an apartment in the palace set apart for the exclusive use of those who happened to be in that state of mind. Such an one shut himself up in this chamber until the fit wore off, or until he was persuaded to be himself again.

The raja refused his evening meal, and as was his wont, when in this frame of mind, retired to the sulking apartment, and lay down. The two elder ranis having been informed of what had occurred, hasted to the raja, and said, "Oh! raja, why are you sulking?" He replied, "This morning a Jugi came to me and said, that if I planted flowering shrubs in my garden the whole city would appear enchanting. If any one will do this work for me, I will rise, if not, I shall remain here." The ranis then addressed him thus, "Oh! raja, rise up, and eat and drink." The raja replied, "Let the young men come to me, I will do as you desire." The two ranis then left, and calling their sons, sent them to their father. Coming into the presence of the raja they said, "Wherefore father are you sulking?" The raja replied, "If you plant flowers in my flower garden I shall be comforted, and shall leave my couch." They said, "Is it on this account you are distressed? We shall cause the garden to be filled with flowers in a short time." On receiving this assurance the raja left his bed, and partook of food, and was refreshed. Lelha's mother now appeared on the scene, and addressing the raja, said, "Wherefore, raja are you sulky?" He replied, "Who told you I was sulky?" She replied, "A shopkeeper gave me the information." Then the raja got angry, and ordered her to leave, but she said, "If you do not tell me why you are sulking I will not depart, am not I also your humble maidservant? Unless you tell me, I will not go, I will die here rather than leave." The raja relented, and related to her all the words of the Jugi. She then returned home.

Her son Lelha entered the house soon after her arrival. He had been engaged in some field sports, and being wearied and hungry, said to his mother, "Give me some cooked rice." She was annoyed with him and said, "Although the raja is ill, your first cry is for boiled rice." Lelha on hearing this went to his father, and enquired what was wrong. But the raja flying into a rage scolded him, saying, "Go away Lelha. What do you want here? Never come near me again. Did not I build a house for your mother and you at the extreme end of the street, away from here? Be off, or I shall beat you." To which Lelha replied, "Oh! father raja, am not I also a son of yours? Let me be foolish or otherwise, still, I am your son, and unless you inform me of what has grieved you, I shall die rather than leave this." Then the raja told him also. He said, "It is because I do not see flowers in the garden." "Oh!" said Lelha, "Is that what distresses you?" He then left.

The raja's four elder sons caused all manner of flowering shrubs and trees to be planted in the garden, and in a short time it was in a blaze of colour, so much so, that the whole city was as if lighted thereby.

Just at this time, when every tree, shrub and plant was covered with blossom another Jugi, named Koema Jugi, came to the city and said to one and another, "You, the citizens of this city, are covering yourselves with renown, but if you attach hiras[2] and manis[3] to the branches, you will add renown to renown." The Jugi's words reached the raja, and he was so much affected by them, that he immediately began to sulk, and on being questioned by his two ranis, he replied, "Do you not remember the words of the Koema Jugi?" They said, "Yes, we remember. He said, 'if you place hiras and manis in this garden the whole country will be resplendent'." "On that account then, I am sulking, and if I do not see hiras and manis, I shall not partake of any food." At the raja's words the two ranis returned sorrowfully to their apartments.

---

[2] Diamonds.

[3] A mythical gem, said to be found in the heads of certain snakes.

At that moment their four sons entered the house and asked for food. The ranis were annoyed, and said, "The raja, your father, is sulking, and you must have food and drink." On learning their father's state the youths were distressed on his account, and went to him weeping, and enquired why he was sulking. He related to them the words of Koema Jugi, and added, "Unless I see hiras and manis attached to the branches of the trees in my flower garden, I shall not rise from my couch." His four sons replied, "Is it for this reason you are grieving? We will search for, and bring them, and if we fail, then sulk again, and refuse your food, and die of hunger, and we will not prevent you, only listen to us this time and get up." The raja was persuaded to rise, and having partaken of food he was refreshed.

II

The raja had planted flowering shrubs in his garden, but the Indarpuri Sadoms[4] ate up all the flowers as they appeared, and so he again began to sulk. He said, "I planted bushes, but I see no flowers. What reason is there for my remaining alive?" And going to the sulking chamber he lay down, and as usual refused to eat. Then there was confusion in the household, and running hither and thither. The two ranis went to him,

---

[4] Celestial horses.

but he was annoyed, and ordered them to leave, saying, "I will not rise, by your telling me," so they returned weeping, each to her own apartment.

Just then their four sons returned from hunting, and demanded food. Their mothers were annoyed, and said, "You young gentlemen are hungry, and must have food, that the raja is sulking is nothing to you, if you are fasting." On hearing this the sons went to their father, and enquired, "Oh! father, wherefore are you sulking?" The raja replied, "Oh! my sons, I am sulking because I see no flowers in my garden. Unless I see flowers in my garden, I shall not remain in this world." His sons replied, "Give us three days, and if at the end of that time you see no flowers, then you may sulk." He was persuaded to rise, and having bathed, and partaken of food, he was refreshed.

Just then Lelha arrived, and addressing the raja said, "Oh! raja, what ails you?" The raja on seeing Lelha was angry, and scolded him severely. He said, "Has Lelha come here? Drive him away at once." Lelha left without uttering another word.

After three days the raja began again to sulk, because there were still no flowers to be seen in his garden. The Indarpuri Sadoms came about mid-night and ate up all the buds. The raja's four elder sons when watching could not remain awake for one hour, and so the

Indarpuri Sadoms came nightly and devoured all the buds that should have burst into flower in the morning, so that not one solitary blossom was to be seen. For this reason the raja again began to sulk, and no one dared to say anything to him.

At this juncture Lelha's mother went from her own house to a shop to buy rice. The shopkeeper refused to supply her. He said, "The raja is sulking, and she comes here to buy rice. I will not weigh it, so go." Lelha's mother went hastily home, and encountered Lelha returning from a stroll. Lelha asked for food. He said, "Oh! mother, give me cooked rice quickly." She rebuked him, and said, "The raja is sulking. The shopkeeper refused to give me rice, how can I give you food? I am a prey to grief, and here my young gentleman is hungry. Go to the raja."

Lelha did as his mother ordered him, and went to the apartment where the raja was, and called several times, "Oh! father, get up." At length the raja asked, "Who are you? Do not irritate me. Go away at once." Lelha replied, "I am your humble slave and son, Lelha." His father said, "Wherefore have you come here? Lelha, Go home, or else I shall beat you. What do you want here? If you go, go at once, if not, I shall have you chastised." Lelha replied, "Because you, Oh! raja, are sulking. The shopkeeper in the bazaar refused to sell to my mother rice, saying, 'something is amiss with the raja, I cannot let you have it.'" The raja then said, "Go, and bring the shopkeeper here." To which Lelha replied, "Why are you sulking? If you do not tell me, it were better for me to die here. I cannot leave you. I have come here fasting, not having eaten anything to-day." The raja said, "Your four brothers have not been able to do anything, and what can I hope from telling you about it, Lelha?" Lelha replied, "It is still possible that I may accomplish something, but although I should not, yet I am a son of yours. Do tell me. If you die, I shall die also. We will depart this life together. I cannot return home." The raja then thought within himself, I will tell him, and let him go. If I do not do so, Lelha may die along with me. Then addressing Lelha, he said, "It is nothing child, only I see no flowers in my garden, and therefore I am sulking. Although your four brothers watched three nights, still I see no flowers." Lelha then said, "If my brothers watched three nights, see me watch one." The raja replied, "Very good my son, let us leave this apartment."

The raja went to bathe, and Lelha going to the shopkeeper bought several kinds of grain, which he carried home and gave to his mother, saying, "Roast a seer of each, and cook some rice for me. I have succeeded in persuading my father to rise. He has bathed and dined, and is refreshed. He was sulking because he can see no flowers in his garden. It was with great difficulty that I prevailed upon him to get up." His mother said,

"What does my Lord want with roasted grain?" Lelha replied, "Let me do with it as I chose, you prepare it. I will take it with me at night when I go to watch in the flower garden." His mother said, "Have you forgotten your brothers' threats to beat you?" Lelha replied, "My brothers may beat me, but no other person. What help is there for it?"

At nightfall, Lelha, having supped, tied up in the four corners of his plaid four kinds of roasted grain, and entering the garden climbed up on a raised platform, and began his vigil.

After a short time he untied one of his parcels of roasted grain, and began leisurely to eat it, one grain at a time. Just as he had consumed the last one, an Indarpuri Sadom descended from the East and alighted in the garden to browse upon the flowers. Lelha seeing it, crept noiselessly up, and laid hold of it, and at the same instant its rider, an Indarpuri Kuri,[5] exclaimed, "Hands off! Lelha. Hands off! Lelha. Touch me not." Lelha replied, to the Indarpuri Kuri, "Besides touching you, I will bind and detain you till morning. You have become bold. You have caused my father to fast; but I have captured you to-night. Where will you go?" "Let me go," she said, "I will bless you." Lelha rejoined, "You are deceiving me." The Indarpuri Kuri made answer,

5 Celestial Maiden.

"I am not deceiving you. I shall give you whatever blessing you may desire. Place your hand upon my head, Lelha." He did so, and a lock of hair adhered to his hand, when he withdrew it. The Indarpuri Kuri then said, "When you desire anything, take that lock of hair into your hand, and say, Oh! Indarpuri Kuri, give me this or that, and instantly you shall receive it. Of a truth it shall be so. I shall never fail you." Lelha then released the Indarpuri Sadom, and it mounted up into the air, and he and his Indarpuri Rider vanished into space.

By the time Lelha had eaten all the roasted grain from another corner of his plaid, another Indarpuri Sadom with his Indarpuri Kuri rider descended from the West. Lelha caught these as he had done the first. This Kuri was a younger sister of the other, and she gave a like blessing to Lelha before he released her horse.

Lelha now began to eat his third parcel of roasted grain, and just as he had finished it he saw another Indarpuri Sadom with an Indarpuri Kuri rider descend from the North, and alight in the garden. Lelha also captured these. The rider was a younger sister of the last. She also gave Lelha a blessing, and was allowed to go.

At cockcrow, Lelha, having eaten the last grain of his fourth parcel, looked up and beheld an Indarpuri Sadom with an Indarpuri Kuri rider descend into the garden from the North. She was the youngest of the sisters. Lelha crept stealthily up, and laid hold of the horse's mane. The Indarpuri Kuri then exclaimed, "Hands off! Lelha. Hands off! Lelha." Then Lelha replied, "You Lelha greatly this morning. It is almost dawn, where can you go to escape punishment?" Then the Indarpuri Kuri said, "Oh! Lelha, We are four sisters, daughters of one mother, I will give you a blessing." Lelha replied, "In this way three persons have fled. You also appear the same." The Indarpuri Kuri said, "We four sisters have one blessing. Place your hand upon my head, and release me." Lelha did so, and the Indarpuri Sadom on being liberated sailed off into the sky with his Indarpuri rider. Lelha tied the four locks of hair of the Indarpuri Kuris each in a corner of his plaid, as he had before done with the roasted grain. When the day fully dawned he returned to his home weeping, for his four brothers seeing the bushes laden with blossom were envious of him, and had hurled him headlong to the ground from off the raised platform on which he sat.

On reaching home his mother said to him, "You see your brothers have beaten you. I warned you against going." Lelha replied, "What help is there for it? My brothers beat me. No one else did. I must bear it." His mother said, "Then, why do you let others know?"

In the morning the raja said, "Last night Lelha was watching. I will go and take a look at the garden." He went and found a perfect sea of blossom, the sight of which almost overcame him.

It so happened that as the raja gazed upon the fairy scene around him, Koema Jugi turned up, and addressing the raja said, "You are lost in wonder, but if you hang hiras and manis on the branches the whole country will be resplendent. Then your wonder and amazement will be increased twentyfold."

III

The raja's garden was without an equal in the world, but the words of Koema Jugi had caused him to become discontented with it, and because there were neither hiras nor manis hanging from the branches he, as before, began to sulk. They reasoned with him saying, "Do not grieve over it. We will bring hiras and manis." So he rose, and having bathed partook of some refreshment.

About this time Lelha's mother went to a shop to purchase food. On seeing her the shopkeeper said, "Something is amiss with the raja, and she is hungry, and comes here giving annoyance. Go away. I will not weigh anything for you." So she returned home empty-handed. As she entered the house she encountered Lelha just returned from hunting, who said, "Oh! mother, give me cooked rice." His mother replied, "Something is wrong with the raja, and here my young lord is fasting, and cries for food. He is greatly concerned about his own affairs."

Lelha went at once to the raja, and enquired "What ails you, father?" The raja replied, "Is there anything ailing me? Has Lelha come here? I will beat him shortly." Lelha said, "Do with me what you please. Why are you sulking? If you do not tell me, although it should cost me my life, I will not leave, rather slay me here at once." The raja thought within himself, "He annoys me, I will tell him to get rid of him." So he said, "Your brothers have gone in search of hiras and manis, and it is because I do not see the trees in my garden adorned with these precious stones that I am sulking. Lelha said, "I will also go." His father said, "Do not go child." But Lelha was determined, and disregarded his father's command.

Lelha went to the bazaar and purchased rice and dal, and his mother when she saw him bringing them home with him, said, "What is wrong? You are completely out of breath." Lelha replied, "My brothers have gone to search for hiras and manis, and I also am busy preparing to follow them." She tried to dissuade him saying, "Although the mean fellows beat you, still you will not keep away from them." Lelha quickly replied, "What help is there for it, mother? Let my brothers beat me or not, what is that to me? I must bear it all." So his mother prepared food, and Lelha, having partaken of it, set out.

He went to the stable, and saddled the lame horse, as his brothers had taken away the good ones, and mounting rode to the outskirts of the city. He then dismounted, and turned the lame horse loose, and went into the raja's flower garden, and said, "Oh! Indarpuri Kuri, give me a horse instantly. My brothers have left me behind, and gone I know not where. Give me such a horse as will enable me to reach them at once." Immediately a horse was at his side, and in a few seconds he was in sight of his brothers. He then alighted from his horse, and said "Oh! Indarpuri Kuri, I return your horse," and instantly it disappeared, and he overtook his brothers on foot.

When his brothers saw him, they said, "He has overtaken us." Some of them said, "Catch him and beat him," others said, "No, let him alone, he will do our cooking. We can go in search of hiras and manis, and leave him to guard our camp. Come let us push on, we have now got a good guard for our camp." This pleased all, and they said, "It is now evening, let us pitch our camp for the night." They did so, and Lelha soon had supper ready, of which having partaken they all retired to rest.

In the morning Lelha again acted as cook, and while it was yet early set breakfast before his brothers, and they having eaten, mounted their horses, and went in search of hiras and manis. They were now a month's journey distant from their own home, and the raja of the country in which they were, had just opened a new bazaar. It was a large and beautiful bazaar, and an Indarpuri Kuri had a stall it. This Indarpuri Kuri had given out, that whoever would go and come twelve kos seven times within an hour should be her husband.

The four sons of the raja, who had come in search of hiras and manis hearing this said, "Some one from amongst us four brothers must marry this girl. Let us exercise our horses, it is possible that some one of them may do the distance in the specified time." They had left home in search of hiras and manis, and now were scheming to secure the Indarpuri Kuri as the wife of one of them. So they returned to camp, and sitting down began to discuss the subject. They said, "If our horses are well exercised, no doubt, but that they will be able to run the distance in the time. Therefore, let us diligently train our horses, so that they may be able to accomplish the task."

While they were thus engaged, Lelha said, “What is it, brothers, that you are discussing?” His brothers rebuked him, saying, “Why are you eavesdropping? We will beat you.” They did not, however, beat him, as they feared he would return home, and leave them without a cook. So he cooked the supper and set it before them, and when they had eaten, they retired to rest.

In the morning Lelha again prepared the food, and his four brothers having breakfasted, mounted and rode off to the bazaar, and there exercised their horses. After they had left Lelha collected all the brass vessels, and what other property there was, and carefully hid them away. Then he called to the Indarpuri Kuri, “Oh! Indarpuri Kuri, give me a horse,” and instantly, just such a horse as he desired stood beside him. He mounted and galloping away soon overtook his brothers. He saluted them, but they did not recognize him. He said to them, “Wherefore, brothers, have you brought your horses to a standstill? Make them race.” They replied, “We were waiting for you. We are tired. It is your turn now.” Lelha immediately switched up his horse, and away it flew at such a pace, that it could scarcely be seen. That day his horse ran twelve kos there and back three times within an hour. At the end of the race soldiers tried to lay hold of Lelha’s horse, but he called out, “Do not touch him. He will not allow you to lay a finger on me." The soldiers said, "The raja has given orders, that the horse that ran three, or five, or seven times is to be brought before him." Lelha replied, "Go, and tell the raja, that the horse bites, so we could not stop him. The raja will not be displeased with you." He then rode away to the camp, and having returned the horse to the Indarpuri Kuri he began to prepare the evening meal, which was ready by the time his four brothers arrived.

After supper they began to talk over the events of the day, wondering who owned the horse that had run so well. Lelha drew near, and said, "What is it, brothers, that you are talking about?" Some said, "Beat him, what has he got to do listening?" Others said, "Do not beat him, he cooks for us." So the matter ended, and all lay down for the night.

In the morning Lelha again prepared the food, and his brothers having breakfasted, mounted their horses, and rode off to the bazaar, where they raced as usual. After they had gone, Lelha gathered all their property together, and hid it as he had done on the day previous. Then, mounting an Indarpuri Sadom, he followed his brothers, and on coming up with them saluted them, but they did not recognize him as their brother. Then a conversation similar to that of the previous day passed between Lelha and his brothers. This time Lelha's horse ran the distance, there and back, five times within the hour. The raja's soldiers again attempted to stop Lelha's horse, but he told them that it was in the habit of biting, so they allowed him to pass, and he galloped off to the camp, and returning the horse to the Indarpuri Kuri began to prepare the evening meal. When his brothers arrived Lelha set food before them, and they ate and drank. After they had supped they sat and talked about the wonderful horse, and its feat that day. Lelha again enquired what they were talking about, but they rebuked him saying, "Do not listen. It is not necessary for you to know what we are speaking about." They all then retired for the night.

Early next morning Lelha set about preparing breakfast, and his brothers, having partaken of it, set out for the bazaar. After their departure Lelha gathered everything together, and hid them as before, and then called upon Indarpuri Kuri for a horse. The horse came, and Lelha mounted and galloped after his brothers. On overtaking them he saluted, and then said, "Wherefore, brothers, do you stand still? Race your horses." They replied, "It is your turn now. We have run, and our horses are tired." Lelha then started his horse, and it ran twelve kos there, and twelve kos back, seven times within the hour. The raja's soldiers again attempted to capture Lelha's horse, but he prevented them, and so returned to the camp. When he had returned the horse to the Indarpuri Kuri he resumed his office of cook, and had supper ready by the time his brothers returned. They sat down together, and began to discuss the wonderful performance of the horse which had that day done the distance seven times in one hour. Lelha again enquired, "What is it that you are talking about, brothers?" Some one said, "Beat him. He has no right to be listening," but another said, "Do not beat him, he cooks our food." When the four brothers were tired talking Lelha set supper before them, and having supped, they lay down to sleep.

Next morning Lelha cooked the breakfast as usual, and his brothers having partaken of it, mounted their horses, and rode off to the bazaar. After they had left Lelha put everything out of sight, as usual. Then he desired the Indarpuri Kuri to give him a horse, and having mounted, he followed his brothers, and on coming near saluted them as before, but again they failed to recognize him.

IV

On the seventh day Lelha again followed his brothers to the bazaar. He begged the Indarpuri Kuri to give him a horse that would do the distance there and back seven times within the hour, and at the end would fall down dead, and also to have another horse ready for him to mount. The Indarpuri Kuri gave him his desire and he rode off to the bazaar, and again saluted his brothers, and at the same time pushed his horse close up to them. They called out, "Keep your horse back, he will crush us." Lelha then enquired why they were standing still. They replied, "We were waiting for you." So Lelha put his horse to the gallop, and did the distance there and back seven times within an hour. On his return the last time the soldiers attempted to lay hold of the horse, but Lelha said, "Let him alone, I will go myself." At the same instant his horse fell, and he leapt from it, and having returned it to the Indarpuri Kuri, he mounted the other, and rode from the race course to the bazaar, and was united in wedlock to the Indarpuri Kuri.

After the marriage he informed his bride that he was in search of hiras and manis for his father's flower garden. She informed him, that lying on the breast of her elder sister, who had been sleeping for twelve years, was a large quantity of hiras. "To obtain them you must first," she said, "buy two bundles of grass, two goats, and a pair of shoes, and make two ropes each two hundred cubits long. My sister is guarded by an elephant, a tiger, and a dog. On entering you will first encounter the elephant, and you must throw him a bundle of grass. A little farther on you will meet the tiger, you must give him a goat. Then you will see the dog, and you must throw him a shoe. When you are returning you must do the same. Throw a shoe to the dog, a goat to the tiger, and a sheaf of grass to the elephant. You must lose no time in possessing yourself of the hiras you will find on my sister's breast. If you delay, her army may take you prisoner." She also said, "My sister's house is situated on an island in a large lake, and you can only reach it by hiring a boat. The door of her house is a large heavy stone, which you must remove before gaining an entrance. On the island there is a Sinjo tree,[6] with branches on the North side, and on the South. On the branches of the South side there are the young of hiras and manis, but on those of the North side there is nothing. On the South side there are five branches, and within the fruit there are manis. Do not forget this. The large hira, which glitters on my sister's breast, is the mother hira." Just as she concluded the foregoing instructions the cock crew, and she added, "See that you remember all I have told you."

Then Lelha left his bride to return to his brothers. As he went he remembered that they would be sure to abuse him for having been absent, so he collected a large number of shells, and stringing them together, hung them round his neck, and went dancing to the camp. When his brothers saw him, in the dress of a merryandrew they rebuked him severely.

---

[6] Ægle Marmelos, Correa.

V

Lelha's excuse for his absence was as follows. He said, "You, my brothers, always leave me here alone in the camp. Yesterday several shepherds came, and forcibly carried me away. They kept me awake all night. They tied these shells round my neck and made me dance. They also made me drive cattle round and round. I had no rest all night. They also shewed me hiras and manis."

Lelha's brothers eagerly enquired, "Where did you see the hiras and manis? Come, show us the place at once." Lelha replied, "We must first buy food for the hiras and manis." So they went to the bazaar to buy food for the hiras and manis. Lelha first bought two goats, and his brothers abused him, and said, "Will hiras and manis eat these?" Some one of them said, "Slap him." Another said, "Do not slap him, they may perhaps eat them." Then he bought a pair of shoes, at which again they reviled him. Then he bought two ropes, when they again reviled him. Lastly he purchased two bundles of grass, and having provided these necessary articles, they went and hired a boat. The horses of the four brothers were dead, so they had to proceed on foot to where the boat lay.

After sailing for some time they reached an island, and landed. They quickly found the house of the Indarpuri Kuri. It was closed by a large stone lying over the entrance. Lelha ordered his brothers to remove it, but they were displeased and said, "How do you expect to find hiras and manis under this stone." Lelha said, "Truly, my brothers, they are under the stone." He pressed them to attempt the removal of the stone, so they, and others to the number of fifty tried their strength but the stone seemed immovable. Then Lelha said, "Stand by, and allow me to try." So putting to his hand, he easily removed it, and revealed the entrance to the mansion of the Indarpuri Kuri. His brothers were so astounded at the strength he displayed that they lost the power of speech.

Lelha then said to his brothers, "Take one of these ropes, and bind it round me, and lower me down, and when you feel me shaking the rope, then quickly pull me up. I go to find hiras." His brothers quickly bound the rope round his body, and he, taking the goats, the pair of shoes, and the bundles of grass, descended.

A short distance from where he reached the ground, he found a door, which was guarded by an elephant bound by the foot to a stake. To him he threw a bundle of grass and passed on. At the next door he found a tiger, likewise chained, and as he approached, it opened its jaws as if to devour him. To it, he gave a goat, and was allowed to pass. At the third door was a dog. He threw a shoe to it, and when the dog was engaged biting it, he passed through. Then he saw the hira sparkling upon the bosom of the sleeping Indarpuri Kuri. Going near, he snatched it up, and fled. The dog, however, barred his exit but he threw the other shoe to it, and passed on. The tiger had devoured the goat he had given to it, and was now alert. To it he gave the other goat, and hurried on. The elephant then opposed him, but the remaining bundle of grass was sufficient to divert his attention, and he passed through the last door. Then violently shaking the rope his brothers speedily hauled him up.

Then they went to their boat, and rowed to another part of the island, where the Sinjo tree grew. They all climbed the tree, but Lelha plucked the five fruits on the branch to the South, while his brothers plucked a large number from the North side.

They then returned to their boat and rowed back to the place from which they had started. From there they went to the house of Lelha's bride. When she heard of their arrival she ordered refreshments to be prepared for them. Her servants also all came, and gave Lelha and his brothers oil, and sent them to bathe. On their return from bathing, their feet were washed by servants, and they were then taken into the house.

After they were seated Lelha's brothers began to whisper to each other, saying, "We do not know of what caste these people are, to whose house he has brought us to eat food. He will cause us to lose caste." Lelha heard what they were saying, and in explanation said, "Not so, brothers. This is my wife's house." They replied, "It is all right then." So they ate and drank heartily, and afterwards prepared to return home.

VI.

The journey was to be by boat. Lelha sent his brothers on ahead in one boat, and he and his wife followed in another. There was a distance of two or three kos between the boats.

Lelha's brothers as they sailed along came to a certain ghat at which a raja was bathing. He was raja of the country through which they were passing. He demanded from Lelha's brothers to know what they had in their boat. They replied, "We have hiras and manis with us." Then the raja said, "Shew them to me. You may be thieves." They replied, "No, they are inside these Sinjo fruits." The raja said, "Break one, I wish to see what they are like." So the brothers broke one, but nothing was found in it. Then the raja called his soldiers, and ordered them to bind the four brothers. So the soldiers seized and bound them, and carried them off to prison. Just then Lelha's boat arrived. He was in time to see his brothers pass within the prison doors. Having seen the four brothers in safe custody the raja returned to the bathing ghat, and seeing Lelha he demanded to know what he had in his boat. Lelha answered, "We have hiras and manis as our cargo." The raja then said, "Shew them to me, I would fain look upon them." Lelha said, "You wish to see hiras and manis without any trouble to yourself. If I show you them, what will you give me in return? There are hiras and manis in this Sinjo fruit." The raja replied, "Those who came before you deceived me. I have no doubt, but that you will do so also." Lelha said, "What will you give me? Make an offer, and I shall shew you them at once." The raja replied, "I have one daughter, her I will give to you, and along with her an estate, if there are hiras and manis in that Sinjo fruit, and if there are none in it, I will keep you prisoner all your lifetime." Lelha immediately broke one of the Sinjo fruits, and five hiras and manis rolled out. When the raja saw it he was confounded, but what could he do? According to his promise, he gave him his daughter and an estate.

The marriage ceremony being over, Lelha was invited to partake of the raja's hospitality, but he refused, saying, "If you set my brothers at liberty I shall eat, but not unless you do so." So the brothers were released, and taken to the bath. After they had bathed, their feet were washed, and they were led into the palace to the feast.

The brothers, after they were seated, began to whisper to each other, saying, "Whose house is this? Of what caste are the people? Does he wish to make us lose our caste?" But Lelha reassured them by saying, "Not so, my brothers. I have espoused the raja's daughter." Hearing this they were relieved, and all enjoyed the marriage feast.

VII

Then they made preparations to continue their journey. Lelha again sent his four brothers first, and he followed with his two wives.

After a sail of a few hours they entered the territory of another raja, and came upon his bathing ghat. The raja was bathing there at the time, and the boat passing, he enquired what her cargo was. The brothers answered, "We have hiras and manis on board." The raja said, "I would see them." They replied, "They are in the boat following us." The raja was displeased with their answer, and ordered them to be seized as vagrants.

Lelha's boat came alongside the bathing ghat just as his four brothers were led off to prison, and the raja seeing it, asked Lelha what cargo he carried. Lelha replied, "Our cargo is hiras and manis." The raja begged Lelha to shew them to him, but he refused saying, "What will you give for a sight of them? Promise something, and you can see them." The raja said, "Of a truth, if you can shew me hiras and manis I will give you my daughter. I have one, a virgin, her I will give you, and I will also confer upon you an estate."

Then Lelha, seizing a Sinjo fruit, broke it, and out rolled five hiras and manis, which when the raja saw he marvelled greatly. He honourably fulfilled his engagement, and Lelha's marriage with his daughter was celebrated forthwith.

The wedding over Lelha was conducted to the bath, and afterwards invited to a banquet; but he declined saying, "So long as you detain my brothers in confinement, I cannot partake of your hospitality." So they were brought to the palace, and their feet bathed, and then ushered into the banqueting room. After they were seated they began to whisper to each other, "What caste do these people belong to, with whom he expects us to eat? Does he intend to make us break our caste?" Lelha hearing them, said, "Not so, my brothers. This is my father-in-law's house." Thus were their doubts removed, and they ate and drank with much pleasure.

VIII

The journey homewards was resumed in the morning, the boats in the same order as previously.

Lelha's four brothers were envious of his good fortune, and on the way they talked about him, and decided that he must be put to death. They said, "How can we put him out of the way? If we do not make away with him, on our return home, he will be sure to secure the succession to our father's kingdom." Having come to this conclusion the next thing was, how could it be accomplished, for Lelha was far more powerful than they were. It was only by stratagem that they could hope to accomplish their purpose, so they said, "We will invite him to a feast and when he stands with a foot on either boat, before stepping into ours, we will push the boats apart and he will fall into the river and be drowned. We must get his wives to join in the plot, for without their aid we cannot carry it into execution." During the day they found means to communicate with Lelha's wives. They said to them, "We will make a feast on our boat. Make him come on board first, and when he has a foot on each boat you push yours back, and we will do the same to ours, and he will fall into the water, and be drowned. We are the sons of a raja, and our country is very large. We will take you with us and make you ranis." Lelha's wives pretended to agree to their proposal; but they afterwards told him all. They said, "Do as they wish, but you will not be drowned. We will remain faithful to you, and you will reach home before us."

So the four brothers prepared a sumptuous feast, and the boats were brought close to each other to enable Lelha and his wives to go on board. One of Lelha's wives tied a knot on his waist cloth, as a token that they would remain true to him. He then preceded them in going into the other boat, and just as he had a foot on each gunwale, the boats were pushed asunder, and Lelha fell into the water. Having thus got rid, as they thought, of Lelha, the brothers made all possible speed homewards.

IX

At the bottom of the river a bell sprang into existence, and Lelha was found lying asleep in it. Then he awoke and sat up, and loosening the knot which his wife had tied on his waist cloth, said, "Oh! Indarpuri Kuri, give me at once food and drink, tobacco and fire," and on the instant his wants were supplied. So he ate and drank, and was refreshed. Then he prepared his pipe, and when he had lit it he said, "Oh! Indarpuri Kuri, give me a fully equipped horse that will carry me home before the tobacco in this pipe is consumed." The last word had scarcely escaped his lips when a horse stood beside him. It was a fierce animal, of a blue colour, and no fly could alight on its skin. It was fully equipped, and impatient to start. Lelha, still smoking his pipe, mounted, and his steed at one bound cleared the river, although it was seven or eight kos broad, and flying like the wind, landed him at home before the tobacco in his pipe was consumed.

The hiras and manis were in the possession of Lelha's wives. His brothers wheedled them into giving them up, saying they will be safer with us.

Lelha went to his mother's house and said to her, "Tell no one of my being here." He had alighted from his horse on the outskirts of the city, and returned it to the Indarpuri Kuri.

A period of ten days elapsed before Lelha's brothers and his wives arrived. The latter declined to accompany the former at once to the raja's palace. They said, "Let your mothers come, and conduct us, as is usual when a bride enters her husband's house." The two elder ranis then came, and the four sons went to the raja's flower garden and hung the hiras and manis on the branches of the trees, and the whole countryside was instantly lighted up by the sheen of the precious stones. The saying of the Koema Jugi was fulfilled to the letter.

Lelha also sent his mother to welcome his wives, but when the elder ranis saw her coming, they reviled her and drove her away. They would not permit her to come near. She returned home weeping. "You told me," she said, "to go and welcome your wives, and I have been abused. When will you learn wisdom?" Lelha ran into the house, and brought a ring, and giving it to his mother, said, "Take this ring, and place it in the lap of one of them." She took the ring, and gave it to one of Lelha's wives, and immediately they all rose, and followed her laughing, to their new home.

The elder ranis went and informed their sons of what had happened, but they said, "They are Lelha's wives. What can we do?"

X

The Indarpuri Kuri whom Lelha had robbed of her hira now awoke, and at once missed her precious jewel. She knew that Lelha had stolen it from her, and summoning her army to her standard marched upon Lelha's father's capital, to which she laid siege, and before many hours had elapsed, the raja was a prisoner in her hands.

This Indarpuri Kuri said to him, “Will you give up the hiras and manis, or will you fight?” The raja sent the following message to his four sons, “Will you fight to retain possession of the hiras and manis, or will you deliver them up?” They were afraid, so they gave answer, “We will not. Lelha knows all about the hiras and manis. We do not.”

The raja then sent and called Lelha, and enquired, “Will you shew fight, Lelha, or will you give up the hiras and manis?” Lelha replied, “I will fight. I will not part with the hiras and manis. I obtained them only after much painful toil, so I cannot deliver them up. Ask them to agree to delay hostilities for a short time, but inform them that Lelha will fight.”

Lelha hurried to the further end of the garden, and taking the hair of the first Indarpuri Kuri in his hand said, “Oh! Indarpuri Kuri. Give me an army four times stronger than the one brought against me, so that I may make short work of my enemies.” Immediately an army of 44,000 men stood in military array, awaiting his orders. The two armies joined battle, and Lelha discomfited the host of the Indarpuri Kuri, and she herself became his prize. She became his wife, and returned no more to her cavernous home in the solitary island. Lelha thus became the husband of four wives.

Then the raja called his five sons together and said, "In my estimation Lelha is the one best qualified to became raja of this kingdom. I therefore resign all power and authority into his hands." Lelha replied, "Yes, father, you have judged righteously. My brothers have caused me much distress. First, they pushed off the raised platform in your flower garden, but of that I did not inform you. Then they caused me, who was the finder of the hiras and manis, to fall into the river. You saw how they refused to fight, and threw all the responsibility upon me. They have used me spitefully. They have tried to make a cat's paw of me."

So Lelha was raja of all the country, and his brothers were his servants. One was in charge of Lelha's pipe and tobacco, another ploughed his fields, and the other two had like menial offices assigned to them.

The Story of Sindura Gand Garur

In a certain village there lived a mother and her son. The boy tended goats in the forest. One day he found a spot of ground, where he thought rice would grow well. So he went home, and asked his mother to give him some seed to sow there. She said, "If you sow rice there it will all be destroyed. The elephants, or the wild jungle cattle, will eat it." But he begged so hard that at length she gave him some seed rice, which he sowed on the small plot of ground in the jungle. It sprang up and grew luxuriantly. Every day he drove his goats there, and spent the long hours in driving the birds and insects away from his little farm.

When the rice had grown to a good height the raja's son with his companion came and set up a mark near by at which they shot with their bows and arrows. The orphan boy was asked to join them, which he did, and so accurate was his aim, that he hit the mark every time he shot. The raja's son and his companion were astonished to see such good shooting, and they said, "The fatherless boy hits the mark every time."

The boy ran home to his mother weeping, and said, "Oh! mother, where is my father?" To keep him from grieving, she told a lie. "Your father," she said, "has gone on a visit to his relations."

The next day after he had again shown great skill with the bow and arrow the raja's son and his companion said, "The fatherless boy hits the mark every time." Hearing this he again went home weeping, and said to his mother, "Oh! mother, where is my father?" She replied, "He has gone to visit his friends." Every day the boy came crying to his mother asking where his father was, so at last she told him. She said, "Your father, child, was carried away on the horns of a Gand Garur[1]."

The boy then said to his mother, "Prepare me some flour. I will go in search of him." His mother tried to

[1] A mythical bird which figures largely in Indian folk lore.

dissuade him, saying, "Where can you go in such a jungle as this?" He, however, insisted, and she prepared flour for him, and he set out.

After travelling many hours he entered the primeval forest, and presently darkness came upon him. After a short time he came to the dwelling of Huti[2] Budhi, and requested permission to pass the night there. This was accorded to him, and he lay down and fell asleep. During the night he was awakened by the Huti Budhi eating his bow and arrows. He called out to her "Oh! old woman, What have you been nibbling at since evening?" The Huti Budhi replied, "It is only some roasted grain, which I brought a while ago from the house of the Chief."

In a short time the nibbling sound was again heard, and he again enquired what she was eating. She returned the same answer as before. "Oh! my son, it is only roasted grain which the chief's people gave me." He did not know that all the time she was eating his bow and arrows.

When morning dawned he requested her to give him his weapons, and on his attempting to string the bow it broke in his hands. The Huti Budhi had eaten the heart

[2] Huti is the name given by Santals to a certain timber boring insect. Budhi is an old woman.

out of the wood, and had left only the outer shell. He left her house planning revenge.

During the day he had an iron bow and iron arrows made. All was iron like the arrow heads. In the evening he returned to sleep at the Huti Budhi's house.

During the night he heard the Huti Budhi trying to nibble his bow and arrows. So he enquired what she was doing. The answer she gave was, "Do you think the Huti Budhi can eat iron."

When morning dawned he demanded his bow and arrows, and received them uninjured, but the lower part of the Huti Budhi's face was all swollen. She had been trying to eat the iron bow and arrows. Her lodger strung his bow, and having saluted her, went his way.

As he journeyed he entered another unexplored forest in the midst of which he discovered a lake, to which all the birds and beasts resorted to quench their thirst. He obtained this information by an examination of its banks, on which he saw the footprints of the various beasts and birds. He now took some flour from his bag, and having moistened it with water made a hearty meal, and then sat down to wait for evening.

As the sun went down the denizens of the forest began to come to the lake to drink. They came in quick succession, and as each made its appearance, he sang assurance to it, that he harboured no evil design against it.

The quail led the way, and to it he sang,
"Oh! quail, you need not fear to drink,

I'll not harm you, I you assure;
But I will slay on this lake's brink,

Cruel Sindura Gand Garur.
He sang in a similar strain to each bird as it came, naming it by its name.

At length the Gand Garur alighted on the edge of the lake to drink, and he at once drew his bow, and sent an arrow to its heart, for he had seen the dried and shrivelled corpse of his father still adhering to its horns. The Gand Garur being dead, he detached what remained of his parent's body from its horns, and taking it in his arms pressed it to his bosom and wept bitterly.

As he wept, Bidi and Bidhati descended from the sky and asked him the reason of his sorrow. So he told them all. They spoke words of comfort to him, and said, "Dip your gamcha cloth in the lake, and cover the corpse with it. And don't you cry, rather bathe and cook some food. And do not cook for one only, but prepare portions for two. And when the food is ready, you partake of one portion, and set the other aside. Then tap your father on the back and say, 'Rise father, here is your food.'" He did as his kind friends bade him, and the dead came to life again. The father sat up and said, "Oh! my son, what a lengthened sleep I have had." The son replied, "A sleep? you must be demented, you were pierced through by the horns of the Gand Garur, and your dried carcase was adhering to them. See I have killed it. It is lying here. Bidi and Bidhati instructed me how to proceed, and I have brought you to life again.

So they returned joyfully home singing the praises of Bidi and Bidhati.

The Tiger and Ulta's Mother

A tiger cub was in the habit of playing under the shade of a certain tree, in which was a crane's nest with a young one in it. The parent cranes brought frogs and lizards to their young one, and what it could not eat it used to throw down to the young tiger, and in this way the two became greatly attached to each other. After a time the tigress died, and left the cub alone in the world. The young crane felt much pity for its afflicted friend, and could not bear the thought of itself being in a better position. So one day it said to the tiger, "Let us kill my mother." The tiger replied, "Just as you please. I cannot say do it, nor can I say do not do it." When the mother crane came to give its young one food, the latter set upon her and killed her. The friendship between the two increased so that they could not be separated from each other. Day and night they spent in each other's society.

After a time the two said, “Come let us make a garden, and plant in it turmeric.” So they prepared a piece of ground, and the crane brought roots of turmeric from a distance. They then discussed the matter as to which part of the crop each would take. The crane said to the tiger, “You, my brother, choose first.” The tiger said, “If I must speak first, I will take the leaves.” Then, said the crane, “I will take the roots.” Having settled this point to their satisfaction, they began to plant. The tiger dug holes, and the crane put in the roots, and covered them over with earth.

A year passed, and they again said to each other, “Which of us will take the roots, and which the leaves?” The tiger said, “I will take the leaves.” The crane replied, “I will take the roots.” So they began to dig up the plants, and cutting the leaves from the roots, placed each by themselves. The tiger collected an immense bulk of leaves, and the crane a large heap of roots. This done each surveyed the other’s portion. That of the crane was of a beautiful, reddish tinge, and excited the envy of the tiger, who said to the crane, “Give me half of yours, and I will give you half of mine.” The crane refused, saying, “I will not share with you. Why did you at first chose the leaves? I gave you your choice.” The tiger insisted, but the crane was obdurate, and before long they were quarrelling as if they had been lifelong enemies. The crane seeing it was being worsted in the wrangle, flew in the face of the tiger, and pecked its eyes, so that it became blind. It then flew away, and left the tiger lamenting its sad fate. Having lost its sight it could not find its way about, so remained there weeping.

One day, hearing the voice of a man near by, the tiger called out, "Oh! man, are you a doctor?" The man stupefied with fear stared at the tiger, and gave no reply. The tiger again said, "Oh! man, why do you not reply to my question? Although you are a human being, have you no pity?" The man then said, "Oh! renowned hero, what did you ask me? I am terror stricken, so did not reply. You may devour me." The tiger replied, "If I had wished to kill you, I could have done so, but I mean you no harm." The tiger again asked the man if he possessed a knowledge of medicine, but he replied, "I do not." The tiger then asked, "Is there one amongst you who does know?" The man replied, "Yes." The tiger enquired, "Who is he?" The man said, "There is a certain widow with two sons, the name of one of whom is Ulta, who possesses a knowledge of medicine, she will be able to cure you." Having given the tiger this information the man went away.

The tiger went to the house of Ulta's mother, and hid himself behind a hedge. He said within himself, "When I hear any one call Ulta then I will go forward." Shortly after the tiger arrived Ulta's mother called Ulta, "Ulta, come to your supper." Then the tiger ran hastily forward, and cried, "Oh! Ulta's mother, Oh! Ulta's mother." But she was afraid, and exclaimed, "This tiger has done for us to-day." The tiger said to the woman, "Do you know medicine?" She replied, "Yes, Wait till I bring it." So hastily running out she said to her neighbours, "A tiger has come to my house. He is blind, and wishes me to cure his blindness." The neighbours said to her, "Give him some of the juice of the Akauna[1] tree. It will increase his blindness." So she quickly brought Akauna juice, and giving it to the tiger, said, "Go to some dense jungle and apply it to your eyes. Do not apply it here, or it will have no effect. Take it away. We are about to sit down to supper, and then my children will go to sleep. The medicine will cause you pain at first, but it will effect a complete cure."

The tiger hurried away to the jungle, and poured the akauna juice into his eyes. The pain it caused was as if his eyeballs were being torn out. He tossed himself about in agony, and at last struck his head against a tree. In a short time, his blindness was gone. He could see everything plainly, and was delighted beyond expression.

One day several traders were passing along a pathway through the jungle in which the tiger hunted. He was lying concealed watching for prey, and when the

---

[1] Calotropis gigantea, R. Br.

traders were passing he jumped out upon them. Seeing the tiger they fled, and left behind them their silver, and gold, and brass vessels. The tiger collected all and carried them to Ulta's mother's house, and presenting them to her said, "All this I give to you, for through you I have again seen the earth. Had it not been for you, who knows whether I should ever have been cured or not." Ulta's mother was delighted with the generosity of the tiger. He had made her rich at once. But she was anxious to get rid of him, and said "Go away. May you always find a living somewhere." So the tiger returned to the jungle again.

Sometime afterwards the tiger was minded to take a wife, and sought his old friend Ulta's mother. On arriving at her house he called out, "Oh! Ulta's mother, where are you? Are you in your house?" She replied, "Who are you?" The tiger answered, "It is I, the forest hero. You cured my blindness." So Ulta's mother came out of her house, and said, "Wherefore, Sir, have you come here?" "I wish you," replied the tiger, "to find a bride for me." Ulta's mother said, "Come to-morrow and I will tell you. Do not stay to-day." So the tiger left.

Ulta's mother then went to her neighbours and said, "The tiger has put me in a great difficulty. He wishes me to find a bride for him." They said to her, "Is he not blind?" She replied, "No. He sees now, and it is that, which distresses me. What can I do?" They said, "Get a bag, and order him to go into it, and then tie up the mouth tightly, and tell him to remain still. Say to him, If you move, or make a noise, I will not seek a bride for you. And when you have him tied securely in the bag, call us." The next day the tiger appeared, and Ulta's mother told him to get into the bag, and allow her to tie it. So he went in, and she tied the bag's mouth, and said, "You must not move, lie still, or I shall not be your go-between." Having secured him, Ulta's mother called her neighbours, who came armed with clubs, and began to beat the helpless animal. He called out, "Oh! Ulta's mother, what are you doing?" She said, "Keep quiet. They are beating the marriage drums. Lie still a little longer." The tiger remained motionless, while they continued to beat him. At length they said, "He must be dead now, let us throw him out." So they carried him to a river, and having thrown him in, returned home.

The current bore the tiger far down the river, but at length he stranded in a cove. A short time afterwards a tigress came down to the river to drink and seeing the bag, and thinking it might contain something edible she seized it and dragged it up on to the bank. The tigress then cut the bag open with her teeth, and the tiger sprang out, exclaiming, "Of a truth she has given me a bride. Ulta's mother has done me a good turn, and I shall remember her as long as I live." The tiger and the tigress being of one mind on the subject agreed never to separate.

One day the two tigers said "Come let us go and pay a visit to Ulta's mother, who has proved so helpful to us. As we cannot go empty handed, let us rob some one to get money to take with us." So they went and lay in wait near a path which passed through the forest in which they lived. Presently a party of merchants came up, and the tigers with a loud roar sprang from their ambush on to the road. The merchants seeing them, fled, and left behind them all their property in money and cloth. Those they carried to Ulta's mother. When she saw the tigers approaching her throat became dry through terror.

Before entering the court-yard they called out to Ulta's mother announcing their approach. Ulta's mother addressed the tiger thus, "Why do you come here frightening one in this way?" The tiger replied, "There is no fear. It is I who am afraid of you. Why should you dread my coming? It was you who found this partner for me. Do you not yet know me?" Ulta's mother replied, "What can you do Sir? Do you not remember that we give and receive gifts on the Karam festival day? On the days for giving and receiving, we give and receive. Now, that you are happily wedded, may you live in peace and comfort; but do not come here again."

The tiger then gave Ulta's mother a large amount of money and much cloth, after which the two tigers took their leave, and Ulta's mother entered her house loaded with rupees and clothing.

The Greatest Cheat of Seven

A great cheat married the cheating sister of seven cheats. One day his father-in-law and seven brothers-in-law came on a visit to his house. After conversing with them for a little, he invited them to accompany him to the river to bathe. He carried a fishing rod with him, and on arriving at the river cast his line into a pool, saying, "Now, fish, if you do not instantly repair to my house, I shall not be able to speak well of you." This he said to deceive the others, as before leaving home he had given a fish to his wife telling her to prepare it for dinner. When seated at table he said to his guests, "the fish we are now eating is the one I, in your presence, ordered to proceed from the river to my house this forenoon." They were greatly astonished at the wonderful properties possessed by the fishing rod, and expressed a desire to purchase it, and offered to pay five rupees for it. He accepted their offer, and they carried the wonderful fishing rod home with them.

Next day they arranged to go a-fishing. They cast the line into a pool as they had seen the cheat do, and said, "Now fish, if you do not repair at once to our home we shall not be able to speak well of you." Having bathed they returned home, and asked to see the fish. Their wives said, "What fish? You gave us no fish. We have seen no fish. Where did you throw it down?" They now knew that their sister's husband was a cheat, so they decided to go and charge him with having deceived them.

The cheat had notice of their coming, and quickly taking his dog with him went to hunt. He caught a hare and bringing it home gave it to his wife, and said, "When we reach the end of the street on our way home from hunting, you make the dog stand near the house with the dead hare in his mouth."

He invited his visitors to accompany him for an hour's hunting, saying, "Come, let us go and kill a hare for dinner." So they went to the jungle, and presently started a hare. The cheat threw a stone at his dog, and frightened it so that it ran home. He called after it, "If you do not catch and take that hare home, it will not be well for you." He then said to his friends, "Come, let us return, we will find the dog there with the hare before us." They replied, "We doubt it much." "There is no mistake about it," he said, "We are certain to find both dog and hare." On reaching home they found the dog standing waiting for them with a hare in his mouth.

His brothers-in-law were astonished beyond measure at the sagacity of the dog, and they said, "Sell this dog to us, we will pay a good price for it." He demanded ten rupees, which they gladly paid. So they returned home, and said nothing to him about his having cheated them in the matter of the fishing rod.

One day, taking the dog with them, they went to hunt. It caught five hares, and its masters were greatly delighted with its performance.

After this the cheat's house was accidentally burnt, and he gathering the ashes together, set out for the bazaar, there to sell them. On the way he fell in with a party of merchants who had a large bag full of silver with them. They enquired what his bag contained, to which he replied, "Gold." They agreed to pass the night in the same encampment, so having partaken of their evening meal, they lay down to sleep. At midnight the merchants rose, and exchanged the bags, and then lay down again. The cheat saw them, and chuckled within himself. In the morning the merchants made haste to leave, as they feared the cheat might find out the theft of his bag. The cheat asked them before they left to help him to lift his bag on to his bullock's back, saying, "It was to receive assistance from you that I encamped here last night." So having helped him to load his bullock they hurried away lest they should be caught. The cheat carried his treasure home, but being unable to count so much money borrowed a measure from his father-in-law, and found he had four maunds of silver.

On returning the measure he sent along with it five seers of silver, saying, "For the ashes of my house I received four maunds of silver, if you reduce your houses to ashes and sell them, you will obtain very much more." So they foolishly burnt their houses, and collecting the ashes went to the bazaar to dispose of them. The merchants to whom they offered them directed them to go to the washermen, saying, "They will possibly buy." But they also refused, and they were compelled to return home without having effected a sale. They vowed vengeance on the cheat, and set out to find him.

When they reached his house the cheat was on the point of starting on a journey. After mutual salutations he said, "I have just killed my second wife. I go to receive eight maunds of silver for her corpse. Dead bodies bring high prices." They said to him, "How about the ashes? We could not sell them." He replied, "You did not go far enough from home. Had you gone to a distance you would have made a good bargain."

The cheat's youngest wife having died he washed the body, and anointed it with oil. He then put it in a large bag, and loaded it on the back of a bullock, and set out. On the way he came to a field of wheat, into which he drove the animal, and then hid himself near by. The owner of the field finding the bullock eating his wheat, beat it unmercifully with a cudgel. The cheat then came from his hiding place, and said, "Have you not done wrong in beating my bullock? If you have killed my wife, where will you flee to? I fell behind, and for that reason my ox got into your field. My wife, whom I have newly married, is weak and unable to go on foot, so I put her into a bag to carry her home on my bullock."

Having opened the bag the wife was found dead, and her assailant stood self convicted of her murder. He gave her husband six maunds of rupees as hush money, so the cheat burnt the corpse and returned home laden with spoil.

The cheat next sent for his brothers-in-law, and shewing them the money, said, "I killed my second wife, and got all this money by selling the corpse." They enquired, "Who are the people who buy dead bodies?" He replied, "They reside in the Rakas country."

Then the seven brothers killed each his youngest wife, and carried the bodies to a distant country to dispose of them. When the people of that country knew the object for which they had come they said to them, "What sort of men are you hawking corpses about the towns and villages? You must be the worst, or else most stupid of men." Hearing this the brothers were dismayed, and began to take in the situation. They perceived that the cheat had again deceived them, and they retraced their steps homewards bitterly lamenting their folly. On reaching their village they cremated the remains of their wives, and from that day had no more dealings with the cheat.

The Story of Two Princesses

A certain raja had two daughters, who were in the habit of amusing themselves out side of the palace walls. One day they saw a crow flying towards them with a ripe Terel[1] fruit in his beak. They then said to each other, "What fruit is it? It looks nice and sweet." The crow let the fruit fall in front of them. They ran and picked it up, and ate it. It tasted deliciously sweet. Then they said, "From whence did the crow bring such a good fruit?" Then they remembered the direction from which they had seen it coming, and said, "If we go this way we shall find it." So they went, but it was only after they had travelled a great distance from home that they found the Terel tree with the ripe luscious fruit.

---

[1] Diospyros tomentosa.

The elder of the two girls climbed up into the tree, and shook down a large quantity of the fruit. They then feasted to their heart's content. Presently they began to feel thirsty, and the elder said to the younger, "You remain here while I go to drink, and I will also bring you water in a leaf cup." Having said this she went away to the tank, and her sister remained under the Terel tree. The day was extremely hot, and they were very thirsty.

The elder having quenched her thirst was returning carrying water for her sister in a cup made of the leaves of a Terel tree, when a bhut came flying along, and fell into the cup of water. Presently she became aware that there was a hole in the bottom of her cup through which all the water had run out. What could she do now? There was no help for it but to return to the tank, make another leaf cup, and filling it with water return to her sister. As she was returning with the cup full of water the bhut again came flying up, and entering the water passed through the leaf, making a hole by which all the water escaped.

Again she made a leaf cup, and having filled it with water was returning when the bhut again came, and destroyed her cup, and caused her to lose the water. In this way she was detained till very late.

A raja who happened to be in the vicinity saw a beautiful girl carrying water in a leaf cup, and a bhut come and make a hole in the cup, so that it soon became empty. Having seen this several times repeated, he drew near, and feasted his eyes on her beauty. Then he carried her away to his palace, where they were joined in wedlock, and the princess, now the rani, cooked the food for herself and her husband.

The younger princess remained near the Terel tree, and although she had given up hope of again meeting her sister, still she continued to wait. At length a herd of Hanuman monkeys came to feed upon the Terel fruit. When the girl saw them coming she was terrified and crept into the hollow of the tree. The monkeys with the exception of an old frail one, climbed into the tree and began to eat the fruit. The old monkey remained below and picked up the fruit shells which the others threw down.

The old monkey having noticed the girl hiding in the hollow of the tree called to the others, "Throw me down some. If you do not I shall not share the Setke chopot I have found." The monkeys in the tree said, "Do not give him any. He is deceiving us. When his hunger is satisfied he will run and leave us." So no fruit was thrown down to him, and he was forced to be content with the shells. The monkeys in the tree having fared sumptuously, left. The old monkey waited till they were out of sight, and then entered the hollow of the tree, where the girl was, and ate her up. He then went to the tank to drink, and afterwards went in the direction of the raja's garden, on reaching which he lay down and died. One of the gardeners finding him dead threw him on the dunghill.

From the place where the monkey decayed a gourd sprang, and grew, and bore a fruit which ripened. One day a jugi, when on his rounds begging, saw this fruit and plucking it took it away with him. Out of the shell he made a banjo, which when played upon emitted wonderful music. The words which seemed to proceed from the banjo were as follows:

Ripe terels, ripe terels, Oh! Sister mine.
Went in search of water, Oh! Sister mine.
Raja and Rani they became.
Seven hundred monkeys old,
Ate me up, ate me up. Oh! Sister mine.

The jugi was greatly pleased with the music of his new banjo, and determined to take it with him when he went a begging. So one day he set out with his banjo the music of which so pleased the people that they gave him large gifts of money and clothes. In course of time he arrived at the palace where the elder sister was now rani, and, being admitted, began to play on his banjo.

The instrument again produced most wonderful music. It seemed to wail as follows:

Ripe terels, ripe terels, Oh! Sister mine.
Went in search of water, Oh! Sister mine.
Raja and Rani they became.
Seven hundred monkeys old,
Ate me up, ate me up. Oh! Sister mine.

Having listened to the music the rani said, "It is wonderfully sweet," and she fancied she heard her sister's voice in every note. She thought it possible that it was she who sang in the banjo, and she desired to obtain possession of it. So she invited the jugi to pass the night in the palace, saying, I would hear more of this entrancing music." The jugi listened to the words of the rani and agreed to remain till morning. So the rani made much of him with the intention of at length obtaining possession of his banjo. She caused a goat to be killed, and she cooked a splendid supper for the jugi, who finding the food so toothsome ate heartily. Wine was not withheld, and the jugi being in a festive frame of mind drank deeply, so that he soon lay as one dead. The rani took the banjo, and placed another in its stead. She then threw filth over the unconscious jugi and retired to her own apartment.

The jugi on awaking before sunrise found himself in a pitiable plight. He felt so thoroughly disgusted with himself that, hastily picking up his staff, cloth, and banjo, he fled with the utmost possible speed from the palace. When dawn broke he saw that the banjo he had was not his own, and although he felt keenly its loss he was too much ashamed of the condition he had been in to go back to seek it.

The rani hid the jugi's banjo in her own room, because she knew her sister to be in it. Whenever the raja and rani went out to walk the girl left the banjo and having bathed and dressed her hair, cooked the family meal, and then returned to the banjo. This happened so often that at last, it came to the knowledge of the raja that a fairy lived in the banjo, and when the way was clear used to come out and prepare food for the rani and himself. So he determined to lie in wait for the fairy cook. He then sent the rani somewhere on an errand, and hid himself in a corner of the room from whence he could see the banjo. In a short time the princess emerged from the banjo, and began to dress her hair, and anoint herself with oil, after which she cooked rice. She divided the food into three portions, one of which she ate. As she was about to re-enter the banjo the raja sprang out and caught hold of her. She exclaimed, "Chi! Chi! you may be a Hadi, or you may be a Dom." The raja replied, "Chi! Chi! whether I be a Dom, or a Hadi, from to-day you and I are one."

Seven Brothers and their Sister

In a certain village there lived seven brothers and a sister. Their family was wealthy. Their father was dead. The brothers agreed to dig a tank so that whatever happened their name would continue. So they began the work, but although they dug deep they found no water. Then they said to each other, "Why is there no water?" While they were speaking thus among themselves a jugi gosae on his rounds, came to the tank in the hope of finding water, but he was disappointed. The seven brothers on seeing the jugi gosae went and sat down near him, and said, "We have been working for many days, and have dug so deep, still we have not reached water. You, who are a jugi gosae, tell us why water does not come." He replied, "Unless you give a gift you will never get water." They enquired, "What should we give." The jugi gosae replied, "Not gold, or silver, or an elephant, or a horse, but you have a sister?" They said, "Yes, we have one sister." He replied, "Then make a gift of her to the spirit of the tank." The girl was betrothed, and her family had received the amount that had been fixed as her price. The brothers argued thus, "We have laboured so long to make a name for ourselves, but have not found water, so where is our name? If we do not sacrifice our sister we shall never obtain the fulfilment of our wishes, let us all agree to it." So they all said, "Agreed," but the youngest did not fully approve of their design.

In the evening they said to their mother, "Let our sister wash her clothes, dress her hair, and put on all her ornaments to-morrow when she brings us our breakfast to the tank." They did not, however, enlighten their mother as to why they desired their sister to be so careful with her toilet.

The following day the mother addressed her daughter as follows, "Oh! my daughter, your brothers yesterday said to me, let the daughter, when she brings us our breakfast come with clean clothes, her hair dressed and all her ornaments on. So as it is nearly time, go and dress, and put on all your ornaments, and take your brothers' breakfast to where they are working." She complied with her mother's order, and set out for the tank, dressed in her best with all her ornaments on, carrying boiled rice in a new basket.

When she arrived at the tank her brothers said to her, "Oh! daughter, set down the basket under yonder tree." She did so, and the brothers came to where she was. They then said to her, "Go bring us water from the tank to drink." She took her water-pot under her arm, and went into the tank, but did not at once find water. Presently, however, she saw the sheen of water in the centre, and went to fill her pitcher, but she could not do so, as the water rose so rapidly. The tank was soon full to the brim, and the girl was drowned.

The brothers having seen their sister perish, went home. Their mother enquired, "Oh! my sons, where is the daughter?" They replied, "We have given her to the tank. A certain jugi gosae said to us, 'Unless you offer up your sister you will never get water'." On hearing this she loudly wailed the loss of her daughter. Her sons strove to mitigate her grief by saying, "Look mother, we undertook the excavation of the tank to perpetuate our name, and to gain the fruit of a meritorious work. And unless there be water in the tank for men and cattle to drink, where is the perpetuation of our name? By our offering up the daughter the tank is full to overflowing. So the cattle can now quench their thirst, and travellers, when they encamp near by and drink the water, will say, 'The excavators of this tank deserve the thanks of all. We, and others who pass by are recipients of their bounty. Their merit is indeed great'." In this way with many such like arguments they sought to allay their mother's grief.

Right in the centre of the tank, where the girl was drowned, there sprang up an Upel flower the purple, sheen of which filled the beholder with delight.

It has already been stated that the girl had been betrothed, and that her family had received the money for her. The day appointed for the marriage arrived, and the bridegroom's party with drums, elephants and horses, set out for the bride's house. On arrival they were informed that she had left her home, and that all efforts to trace her had proved fruitless. So they returned home greatly disappointed. It so happened that their way lay past the tank in which the girl had been sacrificed, and the bridegroom, from his palki, saw the Upel flower in the centre. As he wished to possess himself of it, he ordered his bearers to set down the palki, and stepping out prepared to swim out to pluck the flower. His companions tried to dissuade him, but as he insisted he was permitted to enter the water. He swam to within a short distance of the flower, but as he stretched out his hand to pluck it, the Upel flower, moving away, said, "Chi! Chi! Chi! Chi! You may be either a Dom or a Hadi, do not touch me." The bridegroom replied, "Not so. Are not we two one?" He made another effort to seize the flower, but it again moved away, saying, "Chi! Chi! Chi! Chi! you may be a Dom or a Hadi, so do not touch me." To which he replied, "Not so. You and I are one." He swam after it again, but the flower eluded his grasp, and said, "Chi! Chi! Chi! Chi! You may be a Dom, or you may be a Hadi, so do not touch me." He said, "Not so. You and I are bride and bridegroom for ever." Then the Upel flower allowed itself to be plucked, and the bridegroom returned to his company bearing it with him.

He entered his palki and the cortege started. They had not proceeded far before the bearers were convinced that the palki was increasing in weight. They said, "How is it that it is now so heavy? A short time ago it was light." So they pushed aside the panel, and beheld the bride and bridegroom sitting side by side. The marriage party on hearing the glad news rejoiced exceedingly. They beat drums, shouted, danced, and fired off guns. Thus they proceeded on their homeward way.

When the bridegroom's family heard the noise, they said, one to the other "Sister, they have arrived." Then they went forth to meet the bridegroom, and brought them in with great rejoicing. The bride was she who had been the Upel flower, and was exceedingly beautiful. In form she was both human and divine. The village people, as well as the marriage guests, when they saw her, exclaimed, "What a beautiful bride! She is the fairest bride that we have seen. She has no peer." Thus they all praised her beauty.

It so happened that in the meantime the mother and brothers of the girl had become poor. They were reduced to such straits as to be compelled to sell firewood for a living. So one day the brothers went to the bridegroom's village with firewood for sale. They offered it to one and another, but no one would buy. At last some one said, "Take it to the house in which the marriage party is assembled. They may require it." So the brothers went there, and asked, "Will you buy firewood?" They replied, "Yes. We will take it." Some one informed the bride, that some men from somewhere had brought firewood for sale. So she went out, and at once recognised her brothers, and said to them, "Put down your loads," and when they had done so she placed beds for them to sit on, and brought them water; but they did not know that she was their sister, as she was so greatly changed. Then she gave them vessels of oil, and said, "Go bathe, for you will dine here to-day." So they took the oil, and went to bathe, but they were so hungry that they drank the oil on the way. So they bathed, and returned to the house. She then brought them water to wash their hands, and they sat down in a row to eat. The bride gave her youngest brother food on a brass plate, because he had not approved of what had been done to her, but to the others she gave it on leaf plates.

They had only eaten one handful of rice when the girl placed herself in front of them, and putting a hand upon her head, began to weep bitterly. She exclaimed, "Oh! my brothers, you had no pity upon me. You threw me away as an offering to the tank. You saw me lost, and then went home." When the brothers heard this they felt as if their breasts were torn open. If they looked up to heaven, heaven was high. Then they saw an axe which they seized, and with it they struck the ground with all their might. It opened like the mouth of a large tiger, and the brothers plunged in. The girl caught the youngest brother by the hair to pull him up, but it came away in her hand, and they all disappeared into the bowels of the earth, which closed over them.

The girl held the hair in her hand and wept over it. She then planted it, and from it sprang the hair like Bachkom[1] grass, and from that time Bachkom grass grows in the jungles.

The sister had pity on her youngest brother because he did not join heartily with the others in causing her death. So she tried to rescue him from the fate which was about to overtake him, but in this she failed, and he suffered for the sins of his brothers.

---

[1] Ischœmum agustifolium, Hack.

The Story of Jhore

There was a lad named Jhore, who herded goats, and every day while with his flock he saw a tiger and a lizard fight. The lizard always vanquished the tiger, and the latter after each encounter came to Jhore and said, "Which of us won?" Jhore through fear every time replied, "You won," and the tiger went away pleased.

One day Jhore said to his mother, give me some roasted matkom in a leaf, and put me into a bag and I will tell you something. So she wrapped up some matkom in a leaf, and Jhore crept into the bag and she tied its mouth. Then she said, "What is it, my son, which you wish to tell me?" Jhore replied, "Every day when I am tending my goats I see a tiger and a lizard fight, and the tiger is vanquished by the lizard. The tiger then comes to me and asks, 'which of us won?' Through fear I say, you won, then the tiger goes away satisfied."

While Jhore was relating the foregoing to his mother the tiger was listening at the door, and as he finished his story it rushed in, and seizing the bag carried it off to a dense unexplored forest, on a hill in the middle of which he placed it. Jhore was very uncomfortable, and was considering how he could best free himself from the bag. As he was hungry he was reminded of the matkom he had with him wrapped in a leaf, so he began to open it, and the dried leaf crackled. The tiger hearing the noise, asked what produced it. Jhore replied, “It is yesterday’s lizard.” The tidings of the presence of his mortal enemy so terrified the tiger that he exclaimed, “Stop, stop, Jhore. Do not release him. Let me first escape.” After the tiger left Jhore rolled down the hill side, and away into a still denser forest, in an open spot of which he came to a stop. The fastening of the bag was loosed by this time, and Jhore crawled out. All round this open glade in which our hero found himself was dense forest never trodden by the foot of man, and tenanted by a herd of wild buffaloes. Jhore took up his residence there, and subsisted on the roasted matkom as long as it lasted.

Jhore in his explorations found a number of buffaloe calves left behind by their mothers who had gone to graze. He tended these daily, cleaning the place where they lived, and taking them to the water, where he washed them. In this way a bond of friendship was established between him and the wild buffaloe calves.

Before the buffaloe cows left for their grazing grounds in the mornings the calves said, "You stay away till so late at night that, we are almost famished before you return. Leave some milk with us, so that when hungry we may drink it." So they left a supply of milk with them, which they gave to Jhore. He took such care of his charges that he soon became a great favourite with them.

Matters went on thus for many days till at last the buffaloe cows said among themselves, "We must watch for, and catch whoever it is who keeps our calves so clean." So a very powerful wild buffaloe was appointed to lie in wait, but he missed seeing Jhore when he led the calves to the water and bathed them, and cleaned and swept out their stall. The next day another took his place, but he succeeded no better. The calves were taken to the water, bathed, brought back, and their stall cleaned and swept as usual without his seeing who did it. When the others returned in the evening he informed them that he had failed to solve the mystery. So they said, "What shall we do now? How shall we catch him? Who will watch to-morrow?" A old buffaloe cow replied, "I will accept the responsibility." Hearing her speak thus the others said, "What a good elephant and a good horse could not do, will ten asses accomplish?"

By this they meant, that two of the strongest of their number having failed, this weak old cow could not possibly succeed. However, she persisted, and in the morning the others went to graze leaving her behind.

In a short time she saw Jhore emerge from the dunghill, in which he resided, and loose the calves, and take them to the water. When he brought them back he cleaned and swept their stall, and then re-entered the dunghill. In the evening the others enquired, "Well, did you see him?" The old buffaloe cow replied, "Yes, I saw him, but I will not tell you, for you will kill him." They pressed her, but she refused, saying, "You will kill him." They said, "Why should we kill him who takes so much care of our young ones?" The old buffaloe cow led them to the dunghill, and said, "He is in here." So they called to him to come out, which he did, and when they saw him they were all greatly pleased, so much so that they there and then hired him to continue to do the work he had been doing so well. They arranged also to give him a regular daily supply of milk, so he was duly installed by the herd of wild buffaloes as care-taker of their calves.

Long after this, he one day took his calves to the river and after he had bathed them he said to the buffaloe calves, "Wait for me till I also bathe." They replied, "Bathe, we will graze close by." He having performed his ablutions sat down on the river bank to comb and dress his hair, which was twelve cubits long. In combing his tangled tresses a quantity was wrenched out, this he wrapped up in a leaf and threw into the stream. It was carried by the current a great distance down to where a raja's daughter and her companions were bathing. The raja's daughter saw the leaf floating towards her, and ordered one of her attendants to bring it to her. When the leaf was opened it was found to contain hair twelve cubits in length. Immediately after measuring the hair the raja's daughter complained of fever, and hasted home to her couch. The raja being informed of his daughter's illness sent for the most skilled physicians, who prescribed all the remedies their pharmacopœia contained, but failed to afford the sufferer any relief. The grief of the raja was therefore intense.

Then his daughter said to him, "Oh! father, I have one word to say to you. If you do as I wish, I shall recover." The raja replied, "Tell me what it is, I shall do my best to please you." So she said, "If you find me one with hair twelve cubits long and bring him to me, I shall rally at once." The raja said, "It is well."

The raja caused diligent search to be made for the person with hair twelve cubits long. He said to a certain jugi, "You traverse the country far and near, find me the man with hair twelve cubits long." The jugi enquired everywhere, but could obtain no intelligence concerning him.

They then made up a parcel of flour and gave it to a crow, whom they sent to try and find him. The crow flew caw cawing all over the district, but returned at last and reported failure, saying, "there is not such a man in the world."

After this they again made up a small parcel of flour, and giving it to a tame paroquet, said, "Find a man with hair twelve cubits long." The paroquet, having received his orders, flew away screeching, and mounting high up into the sky, directed his course straight for the unexplored forest. In the meantime the dunghill in which Jhore resided had become a palace.

The paroquet alighted on a tree near Jhore's palace, and began to whistle. On hearing the unusual sound Jhore came out and saw the paroquet who was speaking and whistling. The paroquet also eyed him narrowly, and was delighted to see his hair trailing on the ground. By this he knew that he had found the object of his search, and with a scream of delight, he flew away to communicate the tidings to the raja.

The raja was overjoyed with his messenger's report, and ordered the bariat to set out immediately. In a short time they were on their way accompanied by elephants, horses, drums, and fifes. On reaching Jhore's palace they were about to enter for the purpose of seizing him, when he exclaimed, "Do not pass my threshold." They replied, "We will carry you away with us." He said, "Do not come near." "We will certainly carry you away," they replied. Jhore then ran into his house, and seizing his flute mounted to the roof, and began to play. As the notes of the flute resounded through the forest it seemed to say,

A staff of Pader[1] *wood*
A flute of Erandom[2]
Return, return, return,
Oh! wild buffaloe cows.

The sound of the flute startled the wild buffaloes, and they said one to another, "Sister. What has happened to Jhore?" Then he played again the same as before;

A staff of Pader wood
A flute of Erandom
Return, return, return,
Oh! wild buffaloe cows.

As the echoes of Jhore's flute died away in the forest glades the wild buffaloes sprang forward, and rushed to his assistance. On arrival they found the house and courtyard full of people, and large numbers outside who

---

[1] Stereospermum suaveolens, D. C.
[2] Recinus communis, Linn.

could not gain admittance. They immediately charged them with all their force, goring many to death, and scattering the remainder, who flung away their drums and fifes, and fled as for dear life.

When the raja heard of their discomfiture he sent again for the paroquet, and giving a small parcel of flour to him said, “Stay some time with him until you gain his confidence, and watch your chance to bring away his flute.” Having received his orders he flew off to Jhore’s palace, and having gained access to where the flute was, when Jhore was out of the way he brought it away, and gave it to the raja. The raja was delighted at the sight of the flute, and again ordered the bariat to go to fetch Jhore. A still more imposing array than the former started with elephants, horses, drums, fifes, and palkis, and in due course arrived at Jhore’s residence. On seeing them Jhore called out, “Do not approach, or you will rue it presently.” They replied, “You beat us off the first time, therefore you now crow, but you will not now be able to balk us, we shall take you with us.” Again he warned them to stay where they were, saying, “Do not come near me, or you will rue it presently.” They replied, “We will take you with us this time, we will not leave you behind.” Jhore then ran into his house, and searched for his flute, but as it had been carried away by the paroquet he could not find it, so seizing another he mounted to the roof, and began to play. The flute seemed to say;

A staff of Pader wood
A flute of Erandom
Return, return, return,
Oh! wild buffaloe cows.

The sound startled the wild buffaloes who said one to another "Sister. What is it Jhore says?" Again the music of the flute reached their ears, and the entire herd rushed off to Jhore's rescue. They charged the crowd in and around the palace of their favourite with such determination that in a few minutes many lay gored to death, and those who were so fortunate as to escape threw down drums, fifes, and palkis, and fled pell mell from the place. The raja, being informed of the catastrophe that had befallen the bariat, again called the paroquet, and after he had given him careful instructions as to how he should proceed, dismissed him. He said, "This time you must stay many days with him, and secure his entire confidence and friendship. Then you must bring away all his flutes, do not leave him one." So the paroquet flew swiftly, and alighted on a tree near to Jhore's house, and began to whistle. Jhore seeing it was a paroquet brought it food, and induced it to come down, and allow him to take it in his hand. The two, it is said, lived together many days, and greatly enjoyed each other's society. The paroquet when he had informed himself as to where all Jhore's flutes were kept, one day tied them all up in a bundle, and carried them to the raja. The sight of the flutes revived the drooping spirits of his Majesty. He gave orders a third time for the bariat to go and bring Jhore, so they started with greater pomp and show than before. Elephants, horses, and an immense number of men with drums and fifes, and palkis formed the procession. On their arrival Jhore came out of his palace and said to them, "Do not come near, or you will rue it." They replied, "This time we will have you. We will take you with us." Again Jhore warning them said, "Come no nearer. If you do, you will see something as good as a show. Do you not remember how you fared the other day?" But they said, "We will carry you away with us." Jhore ran inside to get his flute, so that he might call the wild buffaloes to his assistance; but no flute was to be found. Without the help of his powerful friends he could offer no resistance, so they seized him, and bore him away in triumph to the raja.

When the raja's daughter heard of his arrival the fever suddenly left her, and she was once more in excellent health. She and Jhore were united in the bonds of marriage forthwith; but Jhore was kept a close prisoner in the palace.

In course of time a son blessed the union, and when the child was able to walk Jhore's wife said to him, "Where is the large herd of buffaloes which you boast so much about? If they were here "Sonny" would have milk and curds daily." Jhore plucking up courage, replied, "If you do not believe me order a stockade to be constructed thirty-two miles long and thirty-two miles broad, and you shall soon behold my buffaloes." So they made a pen thirty-two miles long and thirty-two miles broad. Then Jhore said, "Give me my old flute, and you all remain within doors." So they brought him his flute, and he went up on to the roof of the palace, and played. The music seemed to call as follows:

A staff of Pader wood
A flute of Erandom
Return, return, return,
Oh! wild buffaloe cows.

The sound startled the wild buffaloes in their forest home, and they said one to another, "Sister. What does Jhore say?" Again the music seemed to say,

A staff of Pader wood
A flute of Erandom
Return, return, return,
Oh! wild buffaloe cows.

At Jhore's second call the herd of wild buffaloes dashed off at their utmost speed, and never halted till they reached the raja's palace. They came in such numbers that the pen could not contain them all, many remained outside.

Those that entered the pen are the domesticated buffaloes of to-day, and those who were without are the wild buffaloes still found in the forests of India.

The Girl who always found helpers

There were once upon a time, six brothers and a sister. The brothers were married. They were merchants, and their business often took them to a distance from home. On such occasions the wives were left alone with their sister-in-law. For some reason or other they hated the girl, and took every opportunity to harass and worry her.

One day when the brothers were away on a journey they said to her, "Oh! girl, go to the forest and bring a load of firewood without tying it." What could the girl do? She must obey her sisters-in-law, or else they would beat her, and give her no food. So she went to the forest with a heavy heart, bewailing her unhappy lot in the following plaintive song,

Woe is me! For I must bring
Unbound a fagot on my head.
Oh! brothers dear, I weeping sing
While business you far hence hath led.

Seeing her grief a Jambro snake asked, “Why daughter, do you cry?” She replied, “My brothers have gone away on business, and my sisters-in-law persecute me. They have sent me to bring a bundle of firewood on my head without tying it.” The Jambro took pity on her and said, “Gather firewood.” Then the Jambro stretched himself full length upon the ground and said to the girl, “Lay the sticks on me.” When she had done so the serpent twined itself round the fagot like a rope, and said, “Now lift it on to your head, but when you reach home, lay your burden down gently.”

When her sisters-in-law knew that she had done what they considered impossible, they were still more angry with her, and ordered her to go to the forest and get milk from a tigress. They gave her a small earthen vessel, saying, “Go, bring us the milk of a tigress.” What could the girl do? She went to the forest with a heavy heart, bewailing her unhappy lot in the following plaintive song,

Woe is me! For I must bring
A brimful cup of tigress' milk
Oh! brothers dear, I weeping sing
While you far hence by trade are lured.

She went to the tiger's den, but only found two cubs, who seeing her sitting weeping at the entrance said, "What are you seeking?" She replied, "My sisters-in-law have sent me to bring some of your mother's milk." The cubs took pity on her and hid her in the cave. They said to her, "Our mother will devour you, so you must not shew yourself." In a short time the tigress returned, and entering the den said, "I smell a human being. Where is he?" The cubs replied, "There is no one here." The cubs milked a little of their mother's milk into the girl's vessel, and when the way was clear they gave it to her, and sent her home.

Her sisters-in-law were greatly disappointed when she brought home the milk, they had expected that the tiger would have devoured her, on that she would return home empty handed, and so give them the opportunity of abusing her for not carrying out their order.

Another day when the brothers were absent they called her, and said, "Go to the forest and bring us some bear's milk." What could the girl do? If she did not do as she was bidden her sisters-in-law would beat her, and give her nothing to eat. So taking the vessel in her hand, she went to the forest, bewailing her unhappy lot in the following plaintive strains;

Woe is me! For I must bring
A brimful cup of she bear's milk
Oh! brothers dear, I weeping sing
While you far hence by trade are lured.

Going to the bear's den she sat down and wept. The she-bear was not in the den, only two cubs were there, who, when they saw the girl, took pity upon her, and asked why she wept. She replied, "My brothers have gone away on business, and my sisters-in-law, who hate me, have sent me to procure bear's milk in order to harass and annoy me." The bear cubs then said, "Our mother will eat you, if she finds you, so we will hide you, and you must keep quiet while she is here." The she-bear on entering the cave said, "I smell a human being." The cubs replied, "There is no one here." The young ones succeeded in obtaining a small quantity of their mother's milk in the girl's earthen vessel, and after the mother bear had left, the cubs dismissed her with their best wishes for her welfare.

Her sisters-in-law were extremely annoyed when she presented the bear's milk to them. They had expected that the bear would have torn her to pieces, or that she would have returned empty handed, and thus give them another chance to abuse and reproach her.

The girl's sisters-in-law again took advantage of their husbands' absence to send her to bring water from the spring in a water-pot with a hole in it. They said, "Go bring water in this water-pot." What could the girl do? She placed it on her head, and went towards the spring bewailing her unhappy lot in the following plaintive song,

Woe is me! For I must bring
Spring water in a leaking jar
Oh! brothers dear, I weeping sing
While business you far hence hath lured.

She seated herself near the well, and exclaimed, "How can I carry water in this pot?" At that moment a frog raised his head above the reeds, and said, "Why do you sit here lamenting?" The girl replied, "My sisters-in-law, who hate me, have ordered me to bring water in this pot which has a large hole in the bottom. How is it possible for me to obey their order?" The frog replied, "Do not worry yourself over it, I will help you." So he pressed himself tightly over the hole, and she filled her pot, and carried it home on her head.

Her sisters-in-law, when they saw her place the water-pot on the ground, full to the brim, were intensely mortified. They had looked for her returning with an empty pitcher, thus affording them an ostensible reason for maliciously upbraiding her.

Another time they scattered a large basketful of Mustard seed on the ground, and ordered her to pick up every seed. They said to her, "You must gather it all into the basket again." What could she do? If she failed they would beat her, entreat her spitefully, and deprive her of food. As she gazed upon the seeds scattered all around her, she bewailed her unhappy condition as follows:

Woe is me! I must refill
This basket with these scattered seeds
Oh! brothers dear, I weeping sing
While business you far hence hath lured.

The plaintive murmur of her song had scarcely died away when a large flock of pigeons alighted near her. They said, "Why do you weep?" She replied, "My sisters-in-law, who hate me, have scattered all this mustard seed on the ground, and have ordered me to pick it all up. One solitary seed must not be left." The pigeons said, "Do not vex yourself, we will soon pick it up for you." As the pigeons were very numerous they soon collected it all into the basket. They did not leave one seed on the ground.

When she called her sisters-in-law to come and see how efficiently the work had been done, they were furious at being again balked by her, and vowed vengeance.

Once again, when the brothers were from home, her sisters-in-law ordered her to go to the jungle, and bring a bale of leaves with which to make the family cups and plates. They said to her, "Go to the jungle and bring a large bale of leaves, but do so without in anyway tying them." What could the girl do? She had been ordered to perform an impossibility. If she refused, or failed to do it, her sisters-in-law would beat her, and deprive her of food. So she went to the forest bewailing her unhappy lot in the following plaintive song;

Woe is me! For I must bring
Of forest leaves an unbound bale
Oh! brothers dear, I weeping sing
While business you far hence hath lured.

As she was sitting in the forest weeping a Horhorang serpent drew near and said, "Wherefore daughter do you grieve?" She replied, "My sisters-in-law hate me and have ordered me to bring leaves without tying them into a bundle. I cannot do this, and I fear their resentment, so I cannot help weeping." The Horhorang said, "Vex not yourself. Go and pluck your leaves and bring them here." She did so, and the Horhorang twined himself round them binding them into a sheaf, which the girl placed upon her head, and carried home.

When her sisters-in-law saw the leaves, and had looked to see that none had fallen by the way they were greatly chagrined. They had expected an opportunity to reproach her with disobedience, and a reason for punishing her.

Although her sisters-in-law had imposed so many impossibilities upon her, yet they had been unable to defeat her. Just at the proper time some one had appeared to help her.

They had seen a bunch of flowers on the top of a high tree, and one day when their husbands were away, they said to her, "Climb up into the tree and pluck the flowers, we wish to dress our hair with them on the occasion of your marriage." No sooner had she clambered up into the tree than her sisters-in-law placed thorny bushes all round in such a manner as to prevent her coming down again. They then went home.

A few days afterwards, the brothers, when returning from a distant market to which they had gone rested for a little under this tree. A tear drop fell on the hand of one of them. Looking at it he said, "Look brothers, this tear drop resembles those of the daughter." Then they looked and saw her high up in the tree. They quickly brought her down, and she related how in time past she had been persecuted by her sisters-in-law whenever they were absent. The brothers were wroth with their wives for having used her so cruelly.

The brothers put their sister into a bag, and carried her home on a bullock's back. When the wives came out to welcome them, they asked, "Where is the daughter?" They gave no reply.

Afterwards the brothers dug a deep well, and on the pretence of propitiating the water spirit induced their wives to stand round the well with offerings of rice, &c., in their hands. At a given signal each hurled his wife head foremost into the well. They then placed a cart over the opening.

In return for the persecution she had endured at their hands, the girl used to go to the well and looking in, say, "You treated me cruelly once, but now, boo sisters boo."

A Simple Thief

Once upon a time a man had some money given to him, and was told to go and buy a foal with it. So he set out to search for one. After a time he came to a village, and going to a house asked the people if they had a foal to sell, as he wished to buy one. They replied, "There are no foals here, but we have mare's eggs. If you will take them we will give them to you." He said, "I will not take eggs, I want a foal." He went to every house in the village asking if they had a foal to sell, but none was to be had; but at each they offered to sell to him mare's eggs.

He then thought within himself, wherever I have gone they have told me that they have not got a foal, but that they can let me have eggs. This being so, why should I give myself any further trouble? I will buy an egg. So he was given a large gourd, and told it was a mare's egg. Having got, as he thought a mare's egg, he joyfully started to return to his home. The man who sold him the gourd informed him, that a foal was certain to be hatched on the way. He was still far from home when the sun set, so he entered a village, and passed the night there. In the morning he set out betimes, and about breakfast time he came to a tank, on the embankment of which he laid down his gourd. He then went into the water to clean his teeth, after which he began to wash his face. While he was thus engaged a jackal came and pushed the gourd down the embankment. The noise frightening the animal it ran away, but the man having caught a glimpse of it called out, "My foal has hatched, and is galloping off." He pursued the jackal, which being terror stricken fled to the jungle, and took refuge in his burrow. The man was pleased to see the creature enter his hole, and he said, "He will soon come out again, and then I shall mount him, and gallop him home." Having said this, he placed himself in such a position that when the jackal came out he could sit down on its back.

He continued standing thus until nightfall, but even then he had no intention of relinquishing his chance of capturing his foal. Late at night some thieves came that way, and seeing him alone in the jungle asked him what he did there. He replied, "I was sent by my friends to buy a foal, but as I could not get one, I bought a mare's egg. I was informed that the egg would hatch on my way home. I spent last night in a village on the way side, and resumed my homeward journey in the morning. On arriving at a tank I laid down my egg on the embankment, and went down into the water, and having cleaned my teeth was washing my hands and face, when the egg hatched and the foal immediately ran away. I followed it, and saw it enter this hole, and I am waiting till it comes out, when I shall mount, and canter it home."

The thieves said, "Leave it alone. Let it remain there. Will you kill yourself for this foal? Come with us, and we will give you a strong, beautiful horse. This one has through fear of you riding on his back gone into this hole. Why should you wait for him? He will stay where he is. Come with us, and we will supply you with a good one presently."

After a little time spent in considering the offer the thieves had made him, he decided to accompany them. The thieves were pleased to receive him into their gang, and at once they proceeded towards a certain village. Having arrived there they went to a rich man's house, and dug a hole through the wall. They then said to our hero of the mare's egg, "You creep in." He raised no objection, but went willingly. They said to him, "Bring out all the heavy articles you can find, they are sure to be the most valuable." When inside he lifted up all he found to test the weight, but nothing seemed to be sufficiently heavy to be worth stealing. He said, "everything is light, what can I take out to them?" At length he came across a millstone, which he pushed through the hole in the wall to his confederates out side. Judging from its weight he expected they would be delighted to receive it, but they said, "Not this, Not this. Bring something worth stealing." So he went back, and finding a drum hanging from the roof he took it down, and began to beat it. When the thieves heard the sound of the drum they decamped, saying, "This fool is certain to betray us to-night." When he brought out the drum to make it over to them, they were nowhere to be seen, so he re-entered the house and placed the drum again where he had found it.

He then saw some milk near the fireplace, and being hungry he determined to cook some food. So helping himself to some rice he began to prepare it by boiling it in the milk. When it was nearly cooked, one of the household turned over in his sleep, saying, "I will eat. I will eat." So he filled a ladle with the boiling rice and milk, and poured it into the sleeper's mouth. The hot food scalded him terribly, and he sprang up howling with the pain.

The other members of the family also jumped to their feet, and laid hold of the intruder, and bound him hand and foot.

When the day broke a large number of people came to see the thief, and began to question him, as to who were his companions. So he related all that had occurred. Then they said, "Of a truth, this man has been the means of protecting us. Had he not acted as he did, we would have been robbed of all we have."

So they loosed his bonds, and set him free. They also allowed him to eat the rice and milk he had cooked, which having done, he went home.